A Lamb's Tale

Written by: Jeannie Bergland

Holly's little lamb

An Interactive Book

To order additional copies of this book, contact:
Xlibris
844-714-8691
www.Xlibris.com
Orders@Xlibris.com

ISBN: Softcover   978-1-6698-7091-3
        EBook   978-1-6698-7092-0

Print information available on the last page

Rev. date: 06/23/2023

Thank you:

God for this story
Holly Williamson for the photo
family and friends who supported me.

Shalom! My name is Ewe, and I have a tale for you.
It started a few thousand years ago
when my ancestors roamed the Earth.
God had created the Earth and everything in it.
It was a beautiful place. All the animals had plenty to eat.
There was a shepherd over us; his name was Adam.
Everyone loved Adam.
One day, one of the little lambs went off with Adam and Eve.
As they walked through the Garden,
Adam was introducing Eve to all the
beauties and wonders in the Garden of Eden.

Draw picture here:

It was a large garden; they walked around for hours.
They stopped for a little while to eat some delicious fruit
and laid down under a tree, looking up and
discussing the beautiful sky, watching a few birds
that flew by, they enjoyed being together.
They soon fell asleep. The little lamb had fallen asleep beside them.
After a while, Eve woke up; she did not want to disturb
Adam, she got up and went for a walk.
The little lamb woke up at Eve's movement and decided to go with her.
Eve and the little lamb were talking, and then Eve
came to a river where two trees stood.
These two trees were different than all the rest.
It was as if there was something supernatural about them.

Draw picture here:

There was a snake in one of the trees; it was
looking right into Eve's eyes.
The little lamb felt like something was transpiring
between Eve and the serpent.
It didn't seem right. So, the little lamb went running back to get Daddy Ram.
Daddy Ram spoke to the little lamb, "Go back to the herd; I will get Adam.
He will know what to do."

Draw picture here:

So, Daddy Ram went to Adam, nudged him gently
with his horns, and woke Adam up.
After Adam noticed Eve wasn't there beside him, he
asked Daddy Ram if he knew where Eve was.
Daddy Ram led Adam to the tree where the snake had been speaking to Eve.
Adam then found her staring at the snake and the forbidden tree.
Adam seemed a bit distracted by Eve's beauty
to even notice the snake in the tree.
He tried to get her attention but could not, and the next thing he knew,
she had taken a piece of fruit off the tree, and then she took a bite!

Draw picture here:

Adam noticed nothing happened to her when she
touched it nor when she took a bite;
he knew that God told them not to eat the fruit from this special tree.
If they were to eat its fruit, then they would die.
No one in the Garden knew what "death" was;
however, they knew it wasn't a good thing.
Since nothing drastically happened to Eve,
she decided to offer the forbidden fruit to Adam.
He thought it must be okay, so he ate it too.

Draw picture here:

Then the serpent hissed in laughter, "Gotcha!"
Daddy Ram saw their faces change before his eyes.
It was like a light had left them; something strange had happened.
Fear now entered the Garden and Death.
Daddy Ram called out to Creator God,
"What can we do to make things right? Something is wrong!"
The serpent hissed back at Daddy Ram,
"Silence! I am in control now! And nothing can stop me!"
The LORD spoke to Daddy Ram,
"The only cure to this problem is an innocent one must die in their place;
because the penalty for eating the forbidden fruit is death."

Draw picture here:

Adam and Eve realized for the first time that they were naked and ashamed.
They worked hard on making coverings for themselves out of fig leaves.
Then God was walking through the Garden to talk with Adam and Eve,
as He did that every evening, but they went and hid
themselves behind some trees.

Draw picture here:

God kept calling out in love waiting for them to respond.
Finally, Adam spoke up and told God they were
hiding because they were naked.
This rebellion broke God's heart. God knew where they were.
God knew they disobeyed; now, Death had access to the whole world.
Daddy Ram ran back to his herd and spoke to them, "Family, something
has happened to our beloved shepherd. He and his wife disobeyed
our Creator; they will die if someone doesn't die in their place.
I know we all love them very much. I have decided
to ask God to let me die for them.
He said that man has sinned; therefore, it must be a man that redeems them.

He did ask if I would be willing to die to cover them,
for they do not have coats like you and I do.
I immediately said, "Yes!"
So, I will be leaving you soon. I love you all."
Then the little lamb asked big Daddy Ram, "Will we ever see you again?"
Big Daddy Ram rubbed up against the little lamb
so warm and gentle and replied,
"I don't know, but I must go."
And so it was that the innocent died.
God made clothes for Adam and Eve, whom everyone loved.
Then Adam and Eve were driven out of the Garden
by an angel with a flaming sword.

Draw picture below:

As time marched on, a baby was born in a manger.
It was a place where animals eat.
He was Jesus Christ, the Lamb of God, who took
away the sin of the whole world.
He was the Innocent One who died for all humanity;
because He was God in the flesh.
God loves all His creation.

Draw picture on this page:

One day, we will all be together without fear, shame, or Death.
One day, we will worship the LORD on a new Earth under a new Heaven.
There will be no more disobedience to our Creator God.
(If we made Jesus Christ Lord of our lives).
That's my tale; it is true. Remember, you heard it first from a little Ewe.

Draw picture:

I told the truth using a made-up story. You can find the true account in the Bible found in Genesis chapter 3 and in Luke chapter 2.

God does love you. Disobedience to His Holy Word is the root cause of all the suffering in our world today. If you want to live with God for all eternity, where there will be no more suffering, please give your life to Him today.

"that if you confess with your mouth the Lord Jesus and believe in your heart that God has raised Him from the dead, you will be saved. For with the heart, one believes unto righteousness, and with the mouth, confession is made unto salvation. For 'whoever calls on the name of the LORD shall be saved.' " Romans 10:9,10,13 NKJV

Printed in the United States
by Baker & Taylor Publisher Services